PLANT PARTS

Why Do

Seeds

First edition.

Celeste Bishop

PowerKiDS press™

New York

Published in 2016 by The Rosen Publishing Group, Inc.
29 East 21st Street, New York, NY 10010

First Edition

Editor: Sarah Machajewski
Book Design: Mickey Harmon

Photo Credits: Cover, p. 22 (dandelions) Brian A Jackson/Shutterstock.com; cover, p. 1 (logo, frame) Perfect Vectors/Shutterstock.com; cover, pp. 1, 3–4, 7–8, 11–12, 15–16, 19–20, 23–24 (background) djgis/Shutterstock.com; p. 5 EM Arts/Shutterstock.com; p. 6 designelements/Shutterstock.com; p. 9 TADDEUS/Shutterstock.com; pp. 10, 17 Nigel Cattlin/Visuals Unlimited/Getty Images; p. 13 (inset) Grygoril Lykhatskyi/Shutterstock.com; p. 13 (main) Edouard Coleman/Shutterstock.com; p. 14 © iStockphoto.com/ClarkandCompany; p. 18 (sky) Evgeny Karadaev/Shutterstock.com; p. 18 (plant) Bogdan Wankowicz/Shutterstock.com; p. 21 oksana2010/Shutterstock.com.

Library of Congress Cataloging-in-Publication Data

Bishop, Celeste, author.
 Why do plants have seeds? / Celeste Bishop.
     pages cm. — (Plant parts)
 Includes index.
 ISBN 978-1-5081-4229-4 (pbk.)
 ISBN 978-1-5081-4230-0 (6 pack)
 ISBN 978-1-5081-4231-7 (library binding)
 1. Seeds—Juvenile literature. 2. Plants—Juvenile literature. I. Title.
 QK661.B57 2016
 575.6'8—dc23
                              2015021405

Manufactured in the United States of America

CPSIA Compliance Information: Batch #BW16PK: For Further Information contact Rosen Publishing, New York, New York at 1-800-237-9932

Contents

Look at this object. Do you know what it is? It's a seed!

A seed is a very important plant part. It is where a plant's life begins.

A seed's hard covering is called a **seed coat**. The seed coat keeps the inside of the seed safe.

seed coat

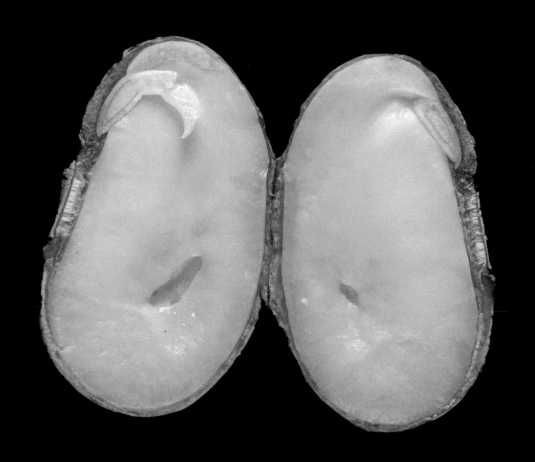

The inside of a seed holds
a baby plant and its food.
A plant needs both to grow.

Some plants form seeds inside their flowers. Other plants form seeds inside their **fruit**.

seeds

13

Seeds are planted in the ground. Seeds need water, sunlight, and air to grow.

What happens when a seed starts to grow? The baby plant breaks out of the seed coat.

17

Parts of the baby plant grow down. These are the **roots**. The rest of the plant grows up.

When the plant is fully grown,
it makes new seeds.

The wind carries seeds to new places. Animals and people can carry seeds, too.
Then, new plants grow!

Words to Know

fruit

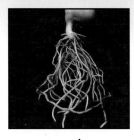
roots

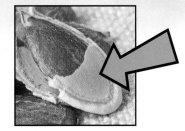
seed coat

Index

Websites

Due to the changing nature of Internet links, PowerKids Press has developed an online list of websites related to the subject of this book. This site is updated regularly. Please use this link to access the list: www.powerkidslinks.com/part/seed

24